CARPET CREATURES

TALES FROM THE DEEP PILE

I0517480

JOANNE SHWED
Storyteller

THOMAS A. EKKENS
Illustrator

Backspace Ink
backspaceink.com

Copyright © 2023 by Thomas A. Ekkens and
Joanne Shwed

ISBN: 978-0-9616675-6-6

Order copies on amazon.com.

Learn about our Carpet Creatures on taegallery.
com/carpet-creatures.

**Read/download the latest version of the Yarn
Scraps Newsletter** on taegallery.com/carpet-
creatures and select "**Link to Yarn Scraps newsletter
(latest edition)**."

My evening routine is to come downstairs, sit in a chair across from my wife Joanne, and discuss today's events and tomorrow's possibilities.

There is a brown carpet on the floor, and the constantly shifting shadows reveal images of faces. Some appear human; others are bestial and even alien.

In the last week of September 2021, I changed the routine by bringing down a sketch pad. I began documenting these creatures by drawing one each evening, sometimes two. As the weeks rolled by, and the entities revealed themselves, I set a couple of rules: no erasures and no tweaking the completed creatures.

These faces percolate to the surface of a 5′ x 8′ fertile area of carpet, tempting my artistic eye. I am the medium through which they emerge, releasing their spirits from the darkness below. Each creature has a story yet to be told.

With the publication of this book, several of these creatures have engaged Joanne to document a slice of their lives with her writing. These stories are the next step in releasing their lost remembrance of what has been or may yet be.

The final and most successful escape from carpet imprisonment is when you read their stories. Then they have truly been released.

—Thomas A. Ekkens

I have never written fiction before. I always wanted to, but I couldn't decide what to write about and never had the confidence to try. Then, unexpectedly and amazingly, these creatures from our carpet inspired me.

When I select a Carpet Creature from our catalog, I look at it for a while and wait for a story—their story—to come through me.

I think about what they might say if they could speak, and I try to imagine what their world might look like, even if it's just for a few minutes.

These stories tell tales of happiness, sadness, despair, pride, fear, success, insecurity, confusion—in other words, life.

Tom and I hope that you will be inspired to play in the sandbox with us and write for our Yarn Scraps newsletter (see page 129). Then, when we get enough material, we'll publish a book.

Most importantly, have fun and be creative!

—Joanne Shwed

CARPET CREATURES

YARN SCRAPS

newsletter information on page 129

1-8

LUIGI LA TELLA

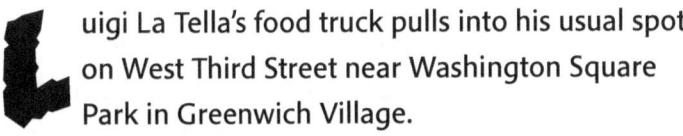uigi La Tella's food truck pulls into his usual spot on West Third Street near Washington Square Park in Greenwich Village.

For over 20 years, he has been there at 11:30 am, every Monday, Wednesday, and Friday, to feed the hungry lunchtime crowd.

On this particular Friday, Luigi's heart jumps with excitement to see the long line waiting for him.

"Luigi!" they cheer as their stomachs growl in anticipation.

With a big wave, he says hello to everyone: *"Ciao a tutti!"*

He smiles, which twists up his moustache at the ends.

Once he is ready to open, he says, *"Salire subito!* Step right up! *Quanti?"*

"One for me, and one for my friend, please."

Today's line is particularly long, and Luigi wonders if he has prepared enough food.

"Oh, well," he thinks, "there's always next time. They'll be back for more."

Luigi's menu is simple: juicy and luscious lasagna, meatballs that melt in your mouth, and bread with just the right amount of butter and garlic. He uses his mother's recipes, passed down from her mother.

When Luigi was a little boy, he watched his mother cook. She would pick him up and place him on the kitchen counter next to her, which was the best seat in the house.

As Luigi serves the last person in line, he thinks about his good fortune:

He has a large family who cares for him.

He has a decent place to live.

His health is good for a man of his age.

He has his own business, which he runs exactly the way he wants.

He is able to do what he loves to do: cook for people.

Luigi's life is simple, like his menu. In his mind, he has it all—except a wife.

Long ago, he was married a few times and always wondered what went wrong. Did all the women leave him for the same reason?

Perhaps they left him because of his smile. When he is angry, he looks like he is smiling—almost like criminals who enjoy watching their victims squirm. Did his smile scare them all away?

When Luigi returns home, he changes into some comfy clothes and snuggles with his beloved cat.

"It's just you and me, Gatta. *Chi ti ama, piccolo mio?* Who loves you, my little one? Are you hungry?"

He heats some leftover meatballs and places them in the kitty's bowl.

"You like that, eh? That's good. *Mangiare* ... eat!"

At the end of the evening, Luigi lies in bed and listens to Gatta purr.

"It sure would be nice if I had some human companionship," he whispers. "Well, *piccolo*, what shall we dream about tonight?"

Gatta gazes into Luigi's eyes. Her whiskers look like a twisted-up moustache, and she seems to be smiling.

11-4

LUCY GOOSY

It was Lucy's 80th birthday, and her party guests were set to arrive very soon. She hurriedly rearranged the worn-out furniture and placed the chips and dip on the unsteady folding table. She dusted off the cobwebs and swept the cat litter under the couch.

Looking in the bathroom mirror, she noticed her shoulder-length, curly gray hair cascading down her head and thought that she looked pretty.

She put on false eyelashes, her reddest lipstick, and a little too much red rouge.

Born Lucille Harris and raised in Lincoln, Nebraska, she had gained the reputation of being "very friendly" to many men. She almost always got their attention and had used their interest as a way to feel accepted. This habit was hard to break, even after she left Lincoln.

In her 20s, she had moved to Los Angeles and tried to capitalize on her good looks by becoming an actress. She got small parts here and there, but no one ever remembered her.

That's when she decided to change her name to Lucy Goosy. She had hoped that her California friends would simply think it was funny and not ask any questions.

Lucy checked the Swedish meatballs—her specialty—that were cooking in the oven, and the clock on the wall caught her attention.

"Oh, my! They'll be here soon. I've got to get ready."

She opened the closet and put on her red, silk dress. She had worn it while playing a geisha in a movie many years ago, and the wardrobe manager had gifted it to her.

"Still fits!" she squealed.

As she walked around the living room, she saw something on the folding table.

"Oh, no ... the balloons!"

Lucy tore open the bag and began to blow. By the fifth exhale, she sat down because she was starting to feel faint.

"Oh, well," she sighed. "I hope no one will mind if we don't have them."

When she regained her strength, she checked the refrigerator and hoped that the beers were cold enough.

"I hope someone brings champagne!"

Trying to calm her nerves, Lucy sat on the couch and looked at the room one more time.

"I'm ready!" she announced to the empty room.

The doorbell rang. She walked to the door and looked out the peephole.

The guests had arrived!

When she opened the door, she was greeted by her smiling friends, and the hugs and kisses commenced.

"Lucy! Thanks for inviting us. You look beautiful."

"Lucy! You *can't* be 80 years old! You look like a teenager."

"Lucy! Your house looks great."

"Lucy! What smells so good?"

Lucy Goosy felt accepted.

She was happy.

17-4

CHESTER MORTON

The memorial of Chester Morton continued with his uncle's words:

"Halloween was Chester's favorite holiday. I'm sure we all remember his wonderful costumes and theatrical talents. This year, he wore a Wookie mask at the Halloween party ... actually, it looked more like Wookie's vagabond cousin."

The crowd giggled softly.

"Chester wished that he could wear a mask on the other 364 days. He felt more relaxed and confident when he was wearing one because no one could see him and judge him."

The crowd nodded silently.

"I remember when Chester was born," his uncle said. "He popped out with lots of hair on his head, and then slowly and steadily grew more.

"Many of the kids at school were brutal. They made ape-like gestures when they passed him accompanied by ape-like sounds. They posted hurtful words on social media and made up stories about him. He cried in his room every night."

The crowd sat quietly.

"As the years went by, Chester's hair kept growing. But, on Halloween, Chester could be anyone he wanted. When he wore the Wookie mask in public this year, the mask hair was automatically accepted and was even entertaining. It was very confusing for him.

"Even so, the Wookie mask quickly became his favorite Halloween costume because, as he told me, 'No one would ever bully a Wookie!'"

The crowd erupted in spurts of laughter as the second speaker came to the podium.

"We are here today to remember Chester Morton. This young man couldn't seem to figure out how to be in this world. He went down the rabbit hole of being born different, experiencing bullying, developing low self-esteem, managing chronic depression, taking a number of medications, having thoughts of suicide, and finally acting on those thoughts. This cycle is a familiar and heartbreaking pattern in our young-adult world today."

A heaviness hung in the room, and the crowd let out a big sigh.

"Chester was my patient. He had a beautiful soul, but he was reluctant to share it with anyone. He had been mistreated for a very long time and had few positive experiences in his short life. I'm sure many of you know what I'm talking about."

The crowd nodded in agreement.

"Doctors walk a tricky tightrope. We use medications to help those who suffer from depression; however, these meds sometimes cause suicidal thoughts in vulnerable patients. This is what happened to Chester."

A few more people spoke (but not Chester's parents), and the memorial came to an end.

As the crowd inched out of the building, they murmured and cried to each other, sharing stories about this young man.

In his own way, Chester had made a huge impact on the community.

As Chester's mother left the church, she took the picture that had been placed beside her son's coffin.

Chester's father trailed behind his wife, his head hung low.

18-1

JASON BIGBY

Jason Bigby once had it all: a wife, a daughter, a dog, a home, a job, a car, and some money in the bank. He was a pretty happy fellow.

Never in a million years did he think that a drunk driver would change it all, but that's what happened.

Jason was the only one who survived the wreck. He was badly hurt and couldn't work. His lost his health insurance, and his medical bills were astronomical.

After a short time, he defaulted on the mortgage payments, which ended in foreclosure, and his home was emptied by the creditors.

He stopped payments on his car, and it was repossessed.

His bank account was almost empty.

Jason's outlook on life shifted. He felt small. Insignificant. Unattractive. Worthless. Unlucky. Sad. He couldn't remember the last time he smiled.

Then, one day, his friend's parents offered him temporary accommodations above their garage, which Jason gladly accepted.

Sitting in the only chair in the small room, Jason thought about his wife, their daughter, and their dog. They were the center of his world. They were his reason for living.

On this chilly morning, without shaving, Jason put on some rumpled clothes and a wooly hat and went outside.

He started walking more quickly than usual.

Before he realized it, he was running very fast and breathing very hard. Down the hill he ran, feeling oddly out of control.

At the bottom of the hill, Jason bent over, put his palms on his knees, and let out a long, loud wail. It was the first time that he had physically grieved since his life fell apart, and it felt good to release it.

Jason asked the trees, "Where shall I go from here? Where *can* I go from here?"

He sat on the ground, eyes closed, and silently wondered.

When Jason returned to the house, his friend's father greeted him.

"Hey, buddy! How are you?"

"Hanging in there, thanks. Just had a good run. How about you?"

"Fine, fine. By the way, my friend is looking for someone to work at his store, which is about a mile away. It's a pet shop, and I know how much you love animals. Even with your injuries, I think you could handle the workload. The pay is not great, but it's something. What do you think? Interested?"

"Absolutely!" Jason answered eagerly.

"Good, good. I'll let him know. Oh, would you like to join my wife and me for dinner tonight? Nothing special."

"That sounds great! Thank you."

Jason took another walk to pick some wildflowers. As he looked around, he noticed the rolling hills, the sun on the flowers, and the snow-capped mountains in the distance. He breathed deeply, taking in as much air as his lungs would allow.

He arrived at dinnertime with flowers in his hand and a big smile on his face.

It turned out to be a very good day.

38-3

MATTHEW GARRETT

atthew Garrett's mouth formed an "O," but nothing came out. It looked like he was singing, but he was frozen and silent.

Officer Johnson put his hand on Matt's shoulder and said, "It's all over now, mister. You're out of danger."

Turning to his partner, the officer whispered, "Ever seen anything like it?"

"No, never. I've been in the force for over 20 years, and this one tops them all."

Matthew sat on the curb and stared at the wreck.

"Good thing I was alone," he thought.

"So, Mr. Garrett, may I ask you some questions about what happened?"

Matthew shrugged his shoulders.

"Can you speak, Mr. Garrett?"

When Officer Johnson received no response, he went to his squad car and came back with a pad and a pen.

"Here you go. Now, what is the last thing you remember before it all happened?"

"S L E E P Y," he wrote.

"So, you were falling asleep?"

Matt nodded.

"What woke you up?"

"S C R E A M S."

"What did you see?"

"D E A D D E E R. D E A D B A B Y."

Matthew put down the pen and looked up at the sky, tears streaming down his cheeks. His eyes were filled with terror, and he was shaking.

The policeman walked a few steps away and called his precinct.

"This is Car 45 on Lake County Road. Officer Johnson. We need a clean-up crew for a deer. We have one infant fatality and one adult female with life-threatening injuries. We have one male adult survivor who seems to have no physical wounds, but he is verbally uncommunicative and appears to be in shock. Over."

"Roger that. On the way. Over and out."

Matthew heard the walkie-talkie, but it sounded like the voices were coming from inside a cave.

He looked at the other car window and saw a woman slumped in the front seat. The windshield was smashed, and glass was everywhere. She wasn't moving.

Matthew's car had hit the back of her car, which was straddling both lanes. He didn't see the car until it was too late.

Several feet in front of the woman's car, a dead deer lay in the road. Matthew's wife had often warned him about the many deer on this dark road and made him promise to be careful.

Matt also saw a baby girl lying across the deer's belly. At first, he didn't understand what he was looking at, but soon it became clear.

He imagined the baby's last, horrifying thoughts.

He thought about the woman who was unaware of the tragedy that awaited her.

Matthew heard the sirens approaching.

He just wanted to go home.

22-9

MISS VY VACIOUS

The strip was quiet that night. There were a few people on the corner of Fifth and Main, but they were walking in the opposite direction of the Moby Dick Inn.

Otto Katzenberger sat in his car across the street. He was expected to go on stage in about a half hour. It was the first time he had ever performed at a drag club in the United States, and he didn't know what to expect.

He had arrived from Germany two weeks before, knowing no one. By chance, he had met a couple of guys who suggested that he audition at the Moby Dick, and he got the gig!

As Otto waited in the car, he tried to calm his nerves. He practiced deep-breathing exercises and thought about the life he left behind.

He remembered his father shouting, *"Was habe ich falsch gemacht?"* ("Where did I go wrong?")

He remembered his mother whispering, *"Du wurdest so geboren, mein Sohn."* ("You were born this way, my son.")

When his mother noticed him wearing her clothes, her face lit up with love as she said, "*Du siehst wunderschön aus!*" ("You look beautiful!")

Now, in the car, Otto thought about his act. He looked at his costume, which was folded neatly on the car seat, and his makeup, including the longest false eyelashes he had ever owned and his trademark cigarette holder.

He was ready.

Otto slowly opened the car door and stepped out. He was wearing flat, comfortable shoes. Actually, he never got the hang of wearing heels. If he wore them for too long, painful blisters would form, and he couldn't walk very well—particularly on stage. He always changed his shoes right before showtime.

He carefully crossed the street, arms full of clothes and everything else he needed, and walked toward the Moby Dick Inn.

He had practiced his English every night before coming to America, and he was able to communicate quite well.

As he opened the bar's front door, he put on his best smile and shouted, "Hello! I'm here!"

The proprietor turned to see who was talking to him. When he saw Otto, he seemed puzzled.

"And you are ...?"

"Miss Vy Vacious from Germany!"

"Ah, yes. Please come in. Your dressing room is in the back."

Otto walked down the dark, dank hallway and saw a sign on a door: "THE TALENT."

He giggled, *"Ich schätze, das bin ich!"* ("I guess that's me!")

In the dressing room, he sat down at the makeshift vanity and looked in the cracked mirror for several minutes.

With his makeup splayed on the table, Otto began to create the image of what he had always wanted to look like. It was a tedious job, but he loved every minute of the process.

When he was done, he stared at his face and said to no one in particular, *"Ich sehe wunderschön aus!"* ("I look beautiful!")

And Miss Vy Vacious surely did.

25-10

JACOB HOFFMAN

I t was a typical day at Alter Cocker Elder Care. At precisely 1 pm—after they had finished their lunch—six of the residents were wheeled into the center of the large recreation room.

They were placed in a circle and sat in silence, each waiting for the first one to talk.

Leah got the ball rolling: "Did you get a load of that horrible meal they served us today?"

After raising what was left of her eyebrows, Eva whined, "Horrible is right. I could show that cook a thing or two about making stuffed cabbage."

Noah added, "My wife used to make potato pancakes. They were so good that they were eaten right off the griddle. These were greasy and too salty."

Benjamin turned to Eva and asked, "And how about that dessert? They call that babka?"

"I used to make babka for my family," Rachel boasted. "There was never any left on the plate."

When Jacob Hoffman first came to the nursing home, everyone was polite and friendly. They tried to get him to talk—or at least smile—but soon they stopped trying.

He just stared into space with a frozen face and a frozen body, day after day. No one looked his way or even tried to communicate with him anymore.

Jacob sat in the wheelchair circle, listening to the comments of the group and silently chuckling as he remembered his wife Esther's terrible cooking.

She would eagerly present him with her recipes of gefilte fish, chicken soup, matzo balls, brisket, and kugel. They all tasted terrible, but he loved her so much that he never said a disparaging word.

She never complained like these people did. She was humble and appreciated him for who he was and for what they had together.

She gave him her love and attention, and he treasured every day that he shared with her.

When he got sick, she was by his side. Once she could no longer care for Jacob, she placed him in this nursing home and died soon afterward.

Even these tender thoughts about Esther didn't change Jacob's frozen existence. He wanted to speak, smile, cry, and laugh, but there was no connection between his brain and his body.

He was a prisoner, enduring a life of silence, unable to express himself ... but he had so much to say!

If he could, he would tell the nursing home residents to show gratitude for the lovely place they all shared.

He would thank the cooking staff for including traditional Jewish food at their dining table.

He would remind everyone to cherish the fact that they were still alive and were able to talk to each other.

The more he thought about it, he realized that there was a reason they were in that nursing home. After all, "alter cocker" is the Yiddish phrase for "old and complaining person."

Jacob knew that he was in the wrong place, but he couldn't tell anyone about it.

83-3

BERTRAM RUFFLE

Bertram Ruffle hadn't left his apartment in a long time. He didn't trim his long, white beard and bushy eyebrows anymore. Why bother?

Over the last 20 years, his weight topped 400 pounds. He needed to go to the doctor, but he couldn't.

He felt claustrophobic in small, enclosed places, like movie theaters and elevators. He had tried many times but ran out, sweating from head to toe.

He disliked open spaces, like parking lots, bridges, and malls, and wouldn't get on a bus, plane, or train. He hadn't visited his family in years, and they kept their visits to a minimum.

Bertram lived on long-term disability payments, due to severe agoraphobia, and supplemented his income with remote computer work. He had not disclosed his disabilities and limitations to his current employer, and he had no intention of doing so.

On this day, his manager scheduled an employee video call, and Bertram declined via e-mail. About 5 minutes later, the phone rang.

"Bertram? This is Mark."

"Oh, hello."

"Everything alright, Bertram?"

"Yes, sir. Thanks."

"We'd like to see you on the video call."

"Well, ..."

"Are your computer and video cam working properly?"

"Yes, they are."

"Well, then, what's the problem?"

"I, ..."

"Bertram, this is not the first time that you've been uncooperative and mysterious. I'm afraid we're going to have to let you go."

"I understand, Mark."

"Is there anything else that you want to say?"

"Uh, ... not really."

"Goodbye, Bertram, and take care of yourself."

He hung up the phone and stared at the floor.

Mark was right. It was not the first time that Bertram had found himself in this situation. In fact, every job had ended this way.

Bertram got all his meals delivered. Every time someone rang the doorbell, his heart pounded. If it wasn't the usual delivery person, he panicked.

The doorbell rang, and it startled him.

He looked through the peephole and saw a woman holding a plastic bag.

"Mr. Ruffle?"

"Yes? What do you want?"

"I have the dinner that you ordered from Bella Italia."

"Leave it by the door, please."

When Bertram could no longer hear the woman's clicking heels on the hallway floor, he opened the door, stuck out his head, and glanced from side to side.

All clear.

He took a deep breath, took one step forward, grabbed the bag, and quickly shut the door.

Bertram's heart was racing.

27-1

YOUMA FAYE

Youma Faye drags her heavy suitcase through the empty train station. It has been a long, hard day, and she is tired and hungry.

She sees a market and goes inside.

A woman behind the counter smiles and says, "I LOVE your headwrap!" She is wearing a similar one in a different color.

"*Parles-tu français?*" Youma asks the woman, thinking that she may know French.

"*Oui, mais parlez-vous anglais?*" The woman speaks French but wants to practice her English.

"*Non, je ne parle pas anglais,*" Youma answers, shaking her head from side to side.

After a few moments of polite French chitchat, there is a heavy pause. The woman looks into Youma's eyes and asks her name.

"*Je m'appelle Youma.*"

The woman reaches across the counter and touches Youma's hand, whispering, "*Youma, as-tu des problèmes?*"

This question takes Youma by surprise. Yes, she has problems—*big* problems—but Youma is unsure if she can trust this kind stranger.

She decides to follow her heart.

The woman takes a break from the market, and they walk to a bar, selecting a booth in the back corner. Youma has never been in such a luxurious place, and it overwhelms her.

They order a drink and something to eat, and Youma tells her story:

"Back home, my friends and I experienced too many instances of male misconduct from teachers and family members, including rape, sexual harassment, and exploitation.

"With financial assistance from my cousin, I fled my homeland and came to America, hoping for a different life. I assumed that men would treat me better in my new home.

"I met an older man in Manhattan who was very kind and generous and, after three weeks, we were living together.

"Slowly, he changed the way he treated me. He started to drink heavily, stay out late, and be physically and verbally abusive. I caught him lying to me, and I smelled perfume on his collar. Of course, he denied it all.

"I had travelled almost 4,000 miles, and history was repeating itself. Now, I am in Grand Central Terminal with my worldly belongings, trying to figure out where to go next."

After the woman listens to Youma's tale, she sighs and whispers, "*Je comprends, Youma.*"

They stroll back to the market, arm in arm.

Before she leaves, the woman turns to Youma and asks gently, "*Iras-tu bien?*"

Youma tells her that, yes, she will be alright.

She knows that there are good men in the world, and she is determined to find one.

47

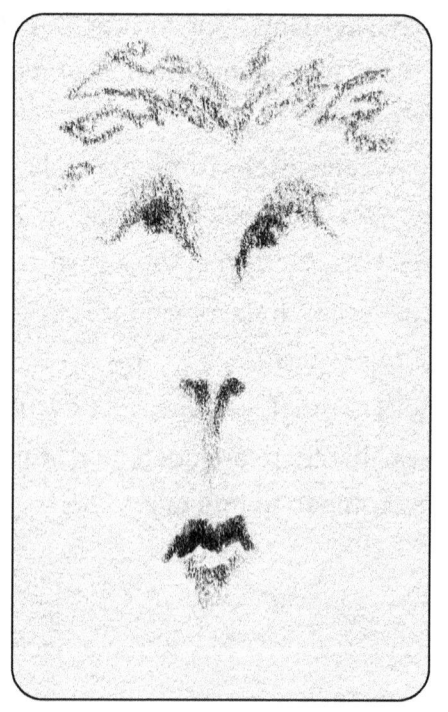

28-9

HAROLD CHASE

Harold Chase looked at everyone with a jaw-set, lips-pursed, don't-mess-with-me attitude. He wore this hard face for most of his life.

The original purpose of this expression was to disarm and ward off the bullies of his youth. However, even though no one had bullied him for many years, his face had never softened.

As Harold walked toward the café near his apartment, he wondered if he would be able to get a seat. Lately, it had been too crowded with too many noisy kids and too many foul-mouthed teenagers. He felt like a cranky, old man—even though he was only 38.

Luckily, Harold found a seat near an open window. He was a people-watcher, but not in a good way. He usually had snarky thoughts about everyone who passed by.

As he looked around the café, he saw a young girl at the next table who was looking right at him.

With a big, toothy grin, she politely said, "Hello, mister!"

"Hello."

"What's your name, mister?"

"Harold Chase."

"My name is Julietta Maya Gibson," she said proudly.

Harold looked down at the menu, wishing that the conversation was over.

No such luck.

"Can I ask you a question, Harold?"

"I suppose so."

"Where is your smile?"

"Huh?"

"Did you lose it somewhere?"

"Lose *what*?"

"Maybe it's under your bed. I've lost *a lot* of things under mine."

"Maybe."

"Maybe your dog hid it. My dog is *always* hiding my things."

"Perhaps."

"I hope you find your smile soon, Harold. I know that you'd have a beautiful smile. *Everyone* needs to smile!"

After a few moments of silent contemplation, Harold raised his head with tears in his eyes.

No one had ever talked to him with compassion and concern, and it felt oddly wonderful.

He paid the check at the front counter and turned around.

Julietta was still looking at him with the same toothy grin.

Their eyes met, and he smiled.

"Bye, Harold!" she said a little too loudly.

As Harold walked to his apartment, he thought about the young girl.

He had felt tenderness from another person, and it felt good.

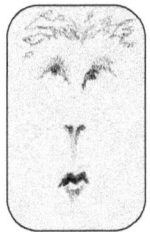

62-5

BUSTER GREEN

otorcycle attorney Buster Green removed the monocle from his right eye and looked at his client, who sat on the other side of his desk.

"Well, ... after looking at this document, it seems as if they have an air-tight case against you."

As the attorney spoke, the client noticed the faint imprint where the eyeglass had been. Buster had lost the string that was attached to the eyeglass, and now he had to be very careful when he wore it.

Buster had a ruddy-looking face because, after all, he rode his motorcycle most of the time.

"So, what are my options, Mr. Green?"

"Well, ... you were recorded by the driver's cell phone. Your license plate number is clearly visible."

"What the hell is going *on* here?" the client barked. "Good Citizens Week? Since when do neighbors rat on each other?"

"Well, ... the driver went to the police station and turned you in," Buster added. "Never heard of anyone doing *that* before."

Buster repositioned his monocle and went back to studying the document.

The ceiling fan made a *whooshing* noise, but it didn't drown out the cars and busses outside.

Buster removed the eyeglass and asked the client to describe the event.

"I was riding my Harley on a lazy, sunny, spring day close to my Malibu home. My headphones were serving up some classic Earth, Wind & Fire, and I was enjoying the warm breeze on my face.

"I approached a stop sign and was idling behind a red Honda Accord. After a few moments, the Honda hadn't moved. I waited a few more seconds, revved my motor, and passed the Honda on the right.

"As I went by, I noticed the driver using a cell phone to record me, but I quickly forgot about it. I rode through the stop sign and went on my way."

After a few moments of contemplation, Buster said, "Well, ... you can't argue with the video. The fine for this violation is $238, plus court costs and assessments. If you are cited for failing to stop under CVC 22450, you will pay the fine, do traffic school, or fight the ticket in court."

Regaining his composure and trying to control his anger, the client stood up and extended his hand

to the attorney, thanking him for his time. He saw
Buster squinting and scrunching his face as he tried
to keep the monocle in place.

Alone in his office, Buster's thoughts returned to
his most pressing problem: the diagnosis of basal cell
carcinoma on the tip of his nose.

His wife had pleaded with him to wear sunscreen
when he was riding his bike, but he didn't listen. Now
he felt like a fool.

His follow-up appointment with the oncologist
was in two hours. The plan was to remove the
cancerous skin and hope that it hadn't gone too deep.

"Well ...," Buster mumbled nervously as he
watched the clock.

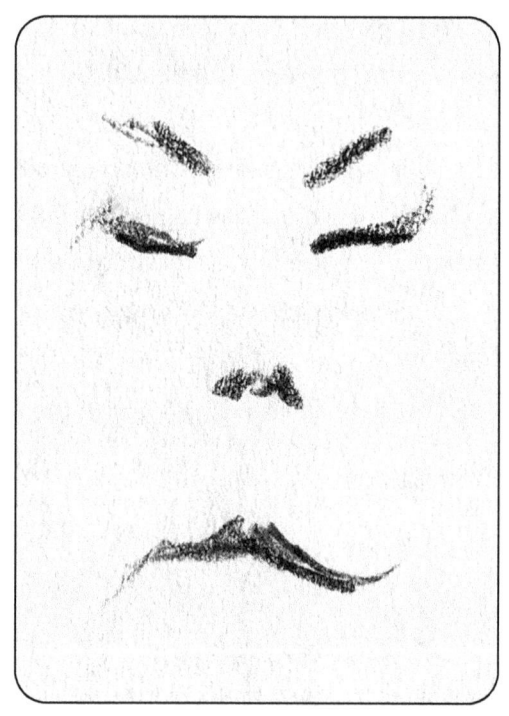

35-3

BOWEN CHENG

Being Peace

If we are peaceful
If we are happy
We can smile and blossom
Like a flower
And everyone
In our family
Our entire society
Will benefit
From our peace
—Thich Nhat Hanh

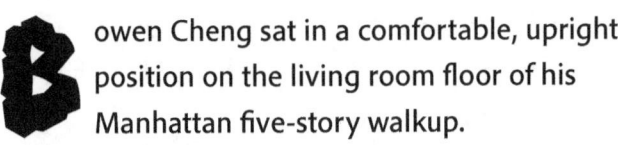owen Cheng sat in a comfortable, upright position on the living room floor of his Manhattan five-story walkup.

He closed his eyes, breathed in and out with his belly, and focused on "zero" rather than on "one."

After a few minutes, Cheng found himself thinking about the family he had left behind in their small village in China. He remembered the day he had told them that he was moving to America.

"Where will your peace be?" they had asked him. "Where will your happiness come from? What is wrong with your life here?"

Cheng's hunger snapped him out of his thoughts, and he navigated the five, long flights to get some lunch. His mouth watered as he thought about all the food choices in his neighborhood.

As he entered Souvlaki's Kitchen, he was greeted warmly by the owner.

"Hey, Cheng! How's it going, man?"

"I'm good, thanks," he responded with a big smile.

"What's on your mind today?"

"I was just thinking about my family. They don't understand why I moved here."

"You came from a small village, right?"

"Yes. Life is quite different there."

"I came from a small town in Greece. You know, New York has its ups and downs, but I wouldn't live anywhere else in the world."

Cheng sat at his favorite table by the window and enjoyed spanakopita and dolmas—their specialty.

Strolling home, he wondered, "Did I make the right decision by moving here? How can a Buddhist live in New York City? Where will I find my happiness and my peace?"

Once inside the front door of his building, Cheng began the long climb up the stairs.

As he turned the corner to start the third flight, he almost bumped into a woman who was coming down.

Their eyes met, and they both burst out laughing.

"Excuse me!" Cheng gasped. "I'm so sorry!"

She waved her long, slender hand and casually said, "No problem. I'm just glad there are some friendly people in the building. I'm new in town."

"Me too," he whispered shyly.

The woman's face looked peaceful and happy.

She finished her descent and stopped at the front door, saying over her shoulder, "I'm Penny. Hope to see you sometime!"

Cheng entered his apartment and resumed his comfortable, upright position on the living room floor.

Things were looking up.

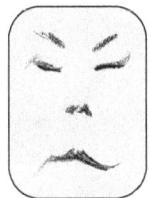

39-4

MRS. GRIMMER

y mind is wandering and wondering about what I will do after school on this hot, summer day, but my beautiful reverie is broken by Mrs. Grimmer's shout:

"SEBASTIAN!"

My seat in the last row of the classroom doesn't protect me as well as I had hoped.

"Yes, Mrs. Grimmer?"

"Are you paying attention, Sebastian?"

Icy chills shoot down my spine as I say, "Yes, Mrs. Grimmer."

"What is the answer to number 4?"

I squirm and look down at my notebook.

"Er ... number 4?"

"Well, class, Sebastian is clearly not interested in what we're doing here, so let's move on ..."

My eyes drift toward the window, and I picture myself swimming in a cool, clear lake—splashing and hollering and laughing and feeling free.

Someone coughs, and my reverie is broken again. I look at the blackboard, and nothing makes sense.

The numbers and letters are jumbled together, and I can't focus. They make my brain hurt.

Number 4? What is she *talking* about? I don't dare ask her. I hope she doesn't call on me again today.

Class dismissed ... *whew*!

After the walk home, I find Mom in the kitchen, and she asks me about my school day.

"Okay, I guess."

"What do you mean, son?"

"Mrs. Grimmer called on me, but I couldn't answer the question."

"Why not?"

"I just couldn't."

"Well," she says as she heads out the door, "you'll just have to try harder tomorrow."

When Dad comes home from work, he gives me a wink, says hello, and sits down to read the newspaper.

What is wrong with me? I read slower than everyone else in my class. I can't concentrate. Clouds are always in my head.

I will try to explain it to Mom and Dad again, but I don't expect anything different to happen. They just think I'm not trying hard enough and it's up to me to fix it.

I sit in my bedroom, staring at my homework, and my reverie returns.

I am swimming in that lake. It is the only place where I don't feel stupid and pointless. Swimming makes me feel happy and calm.

My thoughts drift to Mrs. Grimmer. She has never smiled or said a kind word in our classroom. Her mouth is always in a tight ball, and her steely gaze feels like a knife piercing my heart.

The homework assignment is to write a poem about my hero.

Who is my hero? I guess it's Grandma. She is patient and kind, and I feel special and smart when I am with her. My mind relaxes when she's around, and I can just be myself.

My hero is definitely *not* Mrs. Grimmer.

1-6

BARNEY MCGHEE

After a long, fitful night, Barney McGhee got out of bed without making it. His white, unkempt hair stuck out on the sides, and his scraggly beard framed his weathered face.

He threw on some old, stale clothes, walked down the hill, and slipped into the Better Days Tavern. He was relieved that the bar was almost empty on this melancholy morning.

His favorite barstool beckoned, and he slid into it like an aging home-plate runner.

"The usual," he sighed.

The barkeep gave him a once-over and asked, "How's it goin', Barney?"

"Well, Mary," he whispered, "life feels real hard right now."

"What's troublin' you, my friend?"

"Last night, my ex-wife called to say that our daughter died."

Mary reached across the counter, touched Barney's shoulder, and gave him a little squeeze. What could she say?

She heard the front door open and turned to greet the newcomer.

"Have a seat, sir."

The newcomer ordered a drink and looked at Barney with a big grin.

"How are you this fine morning, chum?"

"I've had better days."

"Oh! I'm so sorry to hear that."

Although Barney wasn't in the mood to talk, he decided to confide in this stranger.

"Maybe it's true that some people are just made the way they are made, and there is nothing anyone can say or do to change them. I threw my life away. I had so much. No one could have loved his family more. I guess I never knew how to show it, even though I treasured each and every sunrise, sunset, star, and moon I ever saw."

The newcomer's smile was gone now.

"Another round?" Mary asked him.

"No, thanks," the newcomer replied as he headed for the door.

Barney thought about the day ahead. What would he do?

He had no passion.

He had no close friends.

He didn't know how to be the person he had always wanted to be.

He wished that he had learned how to have a happy life.

He had so much love to give, but now he felt empty, discouraged, and alone.

"Another round, Mary."

Barney sipped and sighed.

"Sorry to hear about your daughter," Mary said gently. "So ... um ... what do you have planned for today?"

He gave her an old-man shrug and walked outside.

As Barney watched the store owners sweep their sidewalks, preparing for a new day, he looked at the sign above the door: Better Days Tavern.

He hoped that it was true.

50-2

CALEB BOOKER

aleb Booker sat on the front porch of his home on the outskirts of a Wyoming town with a double-barrel shotgun in his lap and a hound dog named Boone at his feet.

"Fine day ... *fine* day. A little warm though. Ain't it, pup?"

Boone looked at Caleb with a how-the-hell-should-I-know expression.

Rocking back and forth in his favorite chair, Caleb gazed at the distant mountains and sighed.

"Used to be crystal clear over there. Now I can hardly see anything at all."

The neighbor's calico sauntered up the front porch steps. Boone nodded politely, quickly lost interest, and went back to licking himself.

Caleb stroked the cat's head and said a few gentle words to her.

He scratched his ankle and noticed that his shoes needed mending.

"Got to get to that tomorrow. Patch up the holes and put some polish on 'em. You never know when company's comin'!"

Caleb chewed on his favorite sandwich: peanut butter, grape jelly, and banana. The jelly dripped on his shirt, and he tried to wipe it off with his fingers. Then he noticed his belly and laughed.

"Yes, sir! Used to have what they call 'six-pack abs.' Don't believe me, Boone? It's a damn *fact*. Drove the girls wild."

He looked at Boone, who was splayed out like a two-bit hooker.

"Being 75 ain't what it's cracked up to be. I've got more hair growing out of my ears and my chin than I've got growing out of my head!"

Caleb sipped on his Coke.

About a mile away, a hawk screamed. Boone's nose pointed to the sound, and he waited. After a few seconds, he slumped back down. That was enough exercise for one day.

"I wonder how Mama's doin'? Got to give her a call tomorrow."

The phone rang in the living room.

"I'll just let the machine get it. Whoever it is, I'll call 'em back."

Actually, Caleb was avoiding several people: his ex-wife, his younger brother, and his daughter. They all had a lot to say, mostly about the way he was living his life. Just a bunch of folks who thought they knew better than he did.

Caleb leaned back and rocked himself to sleep. Before long, he was dreaming of a younger version of himself with six-pack abs and a beautiful girl on each arm.

Boone broke his reverie by yapping at the air.

After a long, satisfying yawn, Caleb stood up and stretched. His back hurt from sitting too much.

"Got to get more exercise ..." he muttered. "They got a gym in town. I'll start next week. Got to get in shape and get those six-pack abs back!"

He turned to his dog and said, "Come on, Boone. Let's go shoot some ducks."

Caleb grabbed his shotgun, walked toward the hills, and whistled.

"Fine day ... *fine* day. A little warm though. Ain't it, pup?"

41-5

BETTY PRINCE

Betty Prince had curly, blond hair and luscious, full lips. Her right eye was perfectly positioned on her face.

Her left eye was another story. People stared at that eye because it was lower, and the eyebrow above it was low too.

There were complications during Betty's birth. The doctor used too much pressure with the forceps, and it caused permanent physical damage.

Of course, Betty didn't consciously remember this event, but the trauma was nonetheless buried deep in her psyche.

Her classmates were often cruel (as kids can be), and they laughed and called her "Quasimodo." As she went from class to class, their mocking gazes burned her soul.

Most days, she would run home and cry to her mother, who would say, "Betty, dear, they don't know what a wonderful person you are. This is not your fault. One day, you'll have people in your life who love you—just the way you are."

Year after year, doctors suggested surgery to improve Betty's flawed facial features, but Betty and her mother were determined to stand up to the bullies, and her mother dedicated each day to teaching Betty how to love herself as she was.

As Betty grew older, she tried to add humor when the subject came up, saying things like, "Well, my face is actually made out of clay. Tomorrow, my right eye will be on my chin!"

She never knew whether the laughter was with her or at her expense, but at least she was trying to deal with it.

One day, Betty was reading a book at the local library and felt someone staring at her.

"Here we go again," she silently gulped. "I thought those days were over."

A soft voice said, "Hello, miss."

Betty looked up and saw a man with a beautiful smile and kind eyes standing in front of her.

"Hello to you, sir!"

"My name is Stanley. I see that you're reading a John Irving novel. Is it *The World According to Garp*?"

"No. Actually, it's *A Prayer for Owen Meany*."

For the next hour, Betty and Stanley talked, and she didn't feel the need to say anything about her left eye.

It was the easiest conversation that she had ever had with another person (except her parents)—no awkward pauses, no judgment, and no stares.

When the library was about to close, Stanley asked Betty to join him for a cup of coffee, and she accepted.

As they walked out of the library, Betty noticed that Stanley limped.

In the coffee shop, Stanley was the one who brought up the subject.

"When I was being delivered, the doctor grabbed my left foot with the forceps because I was turned the wrong way. I guess there was some damage done."

Betty looked at Stanley and smiled.

17-14

THE DARRYLS

L et me tell you what it's like to be smack in the middle of conjoined triplets: It sucks.

Me and my brothers are connected at the head. They know that I am writing this story, but luckily they are asleep right now.

Our folks didn't have the money to separate us when we were born. They are gone now, but we don't want to go through that process and those risks at this late age. We just have to live with it.

I've heard that triplets are uniquely wired, such as having the ability to finish each other's sentences. I've never experienced this bond with my brothers. After all these years, I still don't know what they're going to say most of the time.

Me and my brothers argue until we cross the line. We say hurtful things that hang in the air. Once we're done, there's no door to slam. I can't storm away from the fight. I'm stuck right here—with them.

We all acknowledge that it would be much nicer if we appreciated each other and got along. Trouble is that we've never been taught how to do that. We fall into bad behaviors and usually feel sad and hopeless afterwards.

So far, the tabloids have left us alone. We haven't joined a circus freak show, but it's always a possibility if I can talk my brothers into taking the gig for a little extra cash now and then.

Me and my brothers don't go out much. We're pretty hard to maneuver, and we need a lot of help. We have back problems and other chronic pain. We can't exercise, so we're weak, and our bones are getting more brittle every day.

It's exhausting cleaning ourselves. Wanna talk about going to the bathroom? I'll spare you the details.

We have full bodies with all of the parts. I'm a grown man with sexual urges. Darryl and my other brother Darryl could care less about sex, and neither of them ever talk about it.

One day, I brought up the subject of me having sex with a woman. Their responses were underwhelming:

"Do what you want," Darryl snapped. "We don't really have a choice, do we?"

My other brother Darryl added, "What makes you think you could get someone to do *that* with you?"

I couldn't see their faces when they said these words, but I assume that they were meant to hurt my feelings. Takes the thrill right out of the fantasy, you know?

To be honest, I'm not comfortable doing anything sexual in front of them. That reality is just a little too kinky for me.

It's unbearable to realize that there is no hope of ever having any privacy, or just going somewhere alone, for the rest of my life.

So, here I am: physically connected to two people whom I don't know very well or even like … for eternity.

Shit.

60-5

PROFESSOR ALESSANDRO

Professor Alessandro peeked out of the burgundy velvet curtain. It was almost time to start the biggest and most terrifying magic show he had ever done.

"This crowd is larger than usual," he whispered nervously to no one.

He dabbed his sweaty forehead and closed the curtain behind him.

The professor looked at a heart-shaped mirror on the wall and saw his reflection. Although he was almost 80 years old, his eyes held the twinkle of someone who believed in magic.

"I've still got it!"

In the mirror, he noticed his waxed moustache, curled upward at the ends, which he thought gave him an air of nobility.

His oily hair was dyed black, and his goatee was perfectly groomed—except for a few gray hairs that stuck out like errant wires.

Alessandro heard the thunder rumble close by. Storm clouds hovered overhead, giving him an added sense of fear.

He had never done a magic show in the rain.

He had also never done a magic show without his favorite partner: the purple glove. He had lost it somewhere between here and the last town he visited.

For almost 60 years, the professor's purple glove had travelled with him from town to town, in show after show, and it was always the star attraction.

Alessandro panicked as he heard the thunder come closer. He felt a few raindrops on his face as he peeked out of the curtain again.

"What magic can I share with this large crowd?"

Then he remembered a quote that he had just read but couldn't remember who had said it:

"Music is probably the one real magic I have encountered in my life. It moves. It heals. There's not some trick involved with it. It's pure, and it's real. It communicates and does all these incredible things."

"Aha! That's it!"

The professor closed the curtain and rummaged through his bag.

He found what he was looking for: the silver flute that his grandfather had given him when he was a boy.

His grandfather had also taught him magic, and Alessandro remembered his words:

"If you believe, son, they will too."

He pictured his grandfather's eyes. They were always filled with happiness, love, music, and magic—a beautiful sight for a child to behold.

As the curtain opened, storm clouds moved away.

Professor Alessandro emerged, and the applause was thunderous.

Although he hadn't played the silver flute in many years, it felt good in his hands.

He closed his eyes, put the flute to his lips, and played the song that his grandfather had taught him so long ago.

It was magic.

29-9

DOLLY LANDAU

GET UP

Tweeze and shape eyebrows. Put on false eyelashes. Apply red lipstick. Put on blonde wig. Pencil beauty mark on right cheek.

Dolly Landau finds a gray hair. Another beckoning sign of old age rears its ugly head.

"I was Miss Corn Queen, for crying out loud!" she shouts at the mirror.

Dolly puts down the hairbrush and takes a step back.

"Actually, it's not too bad for an old bag. Not too bad at all."

GO TO WORK

As Dolly pulls into the Red Dog Diner, a man approaches her car.

"Hey, girlfriend. How 'bout a little kiss?"

"Maybe later, honey. Gotta go to work now."

On her break, she looks out the window and sees a truck caravan pulling into the parking lot.

"Here we go," she whispers to no one.

GO HOME

Remove wig. Pin up natural hair. Take off makeup. Climb into bubble bath. Wear fuzzy slippers. Drink wine.

EAT DINNER

Bake chicken. Eat leftover potato salad and pickles. Drink wine. Eat a bag of chocolate chip cookies. Smoke cigarettes. Watch television in flannels.

Dolly thinks about her high school prom date.

"Manfred was crazy about me," she states matter-of-factly. "He stared at me all night at the dance and kept saying how beautiful I was. He treated me like a queen. I wonder whatever happened to him ..."

GO TO BED

Dolly stares at the ceiling. The dreaded nightly thoughts creep into her mind.

"Who am I without my looks? What will people think of me if I'm not pretty anymore?"

She turns on her side and tries to clear her mind, but the thoughts creep back in.

"What do I have to give to anyone?"

Dolly's friends no longer see her soft, happy, gentle smile. These days, her expressions are forced, like the face of someone posing for a picture they don't want taken.

This is a hard time for Dolly. Her mother died, her favorite aunt died, and her best friend died—all in one year.

She thinks about her life, her loneliness, and her own death.

Tossing and turning, she tries to stop these thoughts and get some sleep.

GET UP

Dolly Landau finds another gray hair ...
She is not, as they say, aging gracefully.

58-1

MOSES
MERIWEATHER

From behind the curtain, Moses gazed at the seated spectators who had come to hear his story.

As the room filled and the buzz buzzed, he thought about all that had happened to get him to this place.

"Please be seated," the emcee beckoned to the crowd. "Mr. Meriweather will be speaking in a few moments."

When he got the signal, Moses walked to the armchair and sat down. He felt beads of sweat on his bald head and wished that he had dressed differently.

After unbuttoning his wool jacket and adjusting the microphone, he cleared his throat and began.

"Good evening, everyone. Thank you for coming here tonight. I hope that what I'm about to tell you won't shock you too much."

Murmurs filled the room.

As he waited for silence, Moses stroked his long, gray beard and took a few deep breaths to calm himself down.

"My name is Moses Meriweather," he continued. "I was raised by a tribe in Pawnee, Oklahoma, where I lived a peaceful life with many different types of people. Our days were slow, deliberate, and conscious. We valued the natural world and treated it with respect. We valued each other. We listened to each other. We treasured each other."

Moses was sure that the audience was wondering what piece of information was going to shock them.

"Growing up in Pawnee shaped my life, my thoughts, my morals, my filter, my expectations, my language, my energy, and my gratitude about being alive."

He reached for the glass of water on the table and took a sip.

The audience waited.

"So, what is the shocking thing that I promised to tell you?"

He looked around the room and smiled.

The audience began to smile too, but they were visibly confused.

"Here it is," he announced. "Here's the shocking thing: People CAN live in harmony. In Pawnee, we were not perfect, and we didn't always agree, but we tried to accept each other the way we were.

"Our goal was to get along. Our goal was to allow different points of view. Our goal was to spread love and kindness. Our goal was to be happy.

"*That's* the thing that truly shocks people. They just don't believe that their lives and the world can be this way. My message is that it CAN."

Moses scanned the room and watched the spectators absorb his message.

"Thank you for coming, and good night."

After a smattering of applause, the audience slowly and silently walked out. Their faces displayed a mixture of thoughtfulness and skepticism.

Moses remained in the armchair and stroked his long, gray beard.

"Well, it's a start," he whispered.

6-6

ATHENA JONES

A cloudy day
May 7, 1953

thena Jones struts down the main street of a small town, proudly wearing one of her finest outfits.

She has inherited many of these clothes from her maternal grandmother, and she feels like an important person whenever she wears them.

Her dignified posture and impeccable style set her apart—as if there is a force field around her.

She is a little more than 6 feet tall, which adds to her regal air. She towers over most of the townspeople, casting shadows as she passes.

Her frame is square and solid, and she takes up a large amount of space wherever she goes.

She isn't a traditionally pretty woman, but her face is nonetheless considered beautiful.

No one knows anything about her, and the townspeople often whisper, "Where did she come from? Why is she in our town?"

Her mouth usually looks pouty with down-curved, tightly pursed lips, which raises more questions: "Is she shy? Scared? Arrogant?"

Athena is often alone and avoids eye contact. Occasionally, though, someone will be in her line of sight for a second or two. When this happens, that lucky someone is captivated by her light-blue eyes, but Athena always looks away.

On this May afternoon, Athena walks briskly toward the jazz festival in the park, hoping to get a seat in the front row, so she doesn't have to talk to anyone.

In her haste, she crosses the street and forgets to check for oncoming traffic.

A few seconds later, the townspeople hear a blood-curdling scream and a crashing sound, and all eyes turn to see what has happened.

Athena is lying in the middle of the street, seriously injured but still conscious.

A crowd slowly walks toward her, and a faint murmur spreads among them.

When they reach her body, her mouth is open, as if she has something important to say.

Tears flow down Athena's face. She looks at one person after another and whispers inaudible words to each of them.

The townspeople receive her words in silence.

Athena takes her last breath, and her head falls to the right.

After a few moments, the crowd walks away.

At Athena's funeral, there is no religious service, no one shares their experiences with her, and no family members introduce themselves.

The townspeople stand around the open casket, noticing that her face looks the same as it always did—except for one thing:

Her mouth is finally relaxed.

4-15

EDWARD MILLER

s Edward Miller sits on the park bench, he looks at the big, blue sky and begs, "Help me. Please, please, help me ..."

He is overwhelmed with guilt and grief, and warm, salty tears fill his eyes.

A flock of birds appear in formation, and he wishes that he could join them and fly away.

With eyes closed, Edward mutters to his god for forgiveness, remembering what has happened. Every detail of the event pierces his brain like a knife.

"How could I have *done* this?"

He opens his eyes and walks down the street. He sees his reflection in a store window, and his face looks like he has just witnessed the most horrible and gruesome thing imaginable.

As a matter of fact, he has.

Edward finds a house of worship and goes inside. It is exactly where he wants to be.

After a few moments, he sits down and lets out a long breath.

"How will I be able to explain it? Am I going to jail? What will I tell my family?"

Roused from his reverie, Edward hears a noise and looks up. A tall man is walking down the aisle toward him.

Edward looks at the floor, avoiding eye contact.

The tall man, now standing beside him, whispers, "Rough day?"

Edward keeps his head down.

The tall man lingers beside Edward, waiting for a response.

Edward feels the tall man's steely gaze and, after some very tense minutes, the tall man leaves.

Edward walks down the stairs and into the street. He feels a tap on his shoulder and turns around.

It's the tall man.

"I know what you did," he whispers to Edward.

"You *what*?"

"I know what you did."

"How *could* you? *What* do you know?"

"You can run, but you can't hide," the tall man threatens. "I will make you pay for all of it. You just wait and see."

Edward runs down the street, hoping that the tall man doesn't follow him.

When he looks over his shoulder, the tall man is staring at him, and now he is laughing wildly.

Edward's brain feels like it is going to explode.

"What am I going to do *now*? Where can I hide?"

Edward closes his eyes again.

He will lose everything.

There is no solution.

There is no hope.

When Edward opens his eyes, he is shaking and crying, and his heart is racing.

He can't get the dream out of his head.

63-5

LEONARD FARNSWORTH

eonard Farnsworth's neck was rigid, and he didn't turn his head when he spoke. The only things that moved were his eyes.

One afternoon in his neighborhood bistro, he looked to the right and caught a man and a woman staring at him.

"What are you looking at?" he snapped.

The two people, who were visibly uncomfortable, covered their mouths and whispered, "Should we switch tables? Should we talk to him?"

"I *said*, WHAT YOU ARE LOOKING AT?"

Leonard was not used to his newfound celebrity and had lately felt paranoid, jealous, insecure, and skittish. He assumed that everyone in the room was talking about him.

Sure, he had just opened his new play, but it didn't mean that he had to put up with this intrusion!

"Sorry, Mr. Farnsworth," the woman said sheepishly. "We didn't mean to upset you. We just saw your play, and we loved it!"

"Oh, well ... thank you ... uh, thank you."

Leonard ate the rest of his meal in silence.

After he paid the bill and opened the bistro door, he was met by the fiercest rainstorm he ever had the displeasure of encountering.

"Bugger!" he yelled at the sky. "My new suit and shoes will be ruined."

Leonard had one suit and one pair of nice shoes, which he had bought the week before at a discount store in the dodgy part of town. He had looked over his shoulder every minute, hoping that no one would see him there.

Now he was on his way to the play's opening-night afterparty with ruined clothes. He didn't have time to go home and change. Even if he did, he had no other respectable clothes to wear.

He was a professional playwright now, and he told himself that he had to look the part. Judgment, criticism, lack of privacy, and other unwanted behavior would undoubtedly follow him wherever he went. That was the deal.

Leonard walked on the windy streets—with no umbrella—and asked himself, "Is this what I want for my life? Did I think this through?"

After a few more wet blocks, he arrived at the party and climbed the six slippery stone steps.

As he opened the front door, he looked at his soggy clothes and silently whined, "Oh, no! I look like something the cat dragged in."

Leonard looked up and into the room.

He saw the crowd turn toward him, and a loud wave of applause erupted. Congratulations, encouragement, excitement, compliments, camaraderie, and open affection filled the air.

Leonard was stunned. At no other time in his life were people as gracious, welcoming, friendly, and happy to see him.

"Perhaps I could get used to this," he mumbled as he cautiously joined the party.

40-10

VELMA JACKSON

7:30 am

Velma Jackson takes the long elevator ride up to the 52nd-floor Manhattan office and plops into her chair. She has been running late all morning and is relieved that she has made it to work on time.

She removes her tennis shoes and puts on the high heels that she keeps under her desk.

Her boss hasn't come in yet, so she has a moment to relax.

Her mind wanders to the late 1970s. Fresh out of college, she had joined this firm, thinking that it was as good a place as any.

7:40 am

The phone rings, and Velma snaps back to the present day.

She is 56 now.

"Velma," her boss says, "please bring me the Pensky file ..."

"Will do."

"... and please join us for the meeting."

As Velma enters the conference room, she looks different than the rest of the team. Everyone notices—and not for the first time.

Her hair is spiked at the top like a mohawk and shaved on both sides. She has stretched-out earlobes with big holes in them. Her eyebrows are plucked thin and shaped with a dark pencil. Her lipstick is dark brown, which emphasizes her full lips.

She stands out.

8 am

The meeting is over, and everyone heads back to their desks. As Velma passes the breakroom, she overhears an ongoing conversation.

"Did you see Velma's latest hairdo? What does she think she is—a punk rocker?"

"Yeah, I know. She has no place at this company. We have a reputation and an image to uphold. Don't we?"

"She's too fat to dress like that. It's so unbecoming. Doesn't she have any dignity?"

8:15 am

Velma is quite upset after hearing this nasty, trivial gossip.

Back at her desk, her mind rages: "What about all my hard work? What about my dedication to this company? I thought these people were my friends."

She puts on her tennis shoes and heads for the subway, talking to no one and making no eye contact.

8:46 am

Someone in the office hears a crash.

9:03 am

Velma Jackson sits on her living room couch and stares at the television.

Her glazed eyes watch the second tower fall.

67-7

MARJORIE EVENINGSTAR

As Marjorie Eveningstar stood behind the white, gossamer curtain in the doorway, she peeked into the large, crowded dance hall. She felt the curtain on her face as it played with the summer breeze.

She had put on her best false eyelashes and her reddest lipstick—and even plucked her eyebrows—before coming here.

She was ready.

After taking a deep breath, Marjorie walked into the dance hall. Beads of sweat formed all over her body, and her makeup felt oozy.

"Get it together, girl!" she told herself.

Marjorie heard a voice from behind, asking, "Would you like to dance?"

When she spun around, she was pleased to see a man who lived in her neighborhood.

"Yes, I'd *love* to!"

The man took her in his arms, and it was magical. There was a comfortable feeling between them even though they had never talked before.

"What is your name?"

"Marjorie Eveningstar."

"You dance like a dream, my dear."

"And you are the most confident and smoothest dancer I've ever had the pleasure of dancing with, sir."

They couldn't stop staring at each other. Their bodies buzzed with excitement, ease, and joy. Dance after dance, they glided as one and felt weightless.

At the end of the night, they knew something wonderful had happened, and they didn't want it to end.

The man took Marjorie's hand and walked her home in silence. When they got to her door, he turned and looked into her eyes.

"I've seen you many times," he said softly, "but I was always too nervous to talk to you. Meeting you tonight was a lucky break. I got up the nerve to ask you to dance, and you said yes."

Marjorie returned his look and added, "I've seen you many times too. I almost didn't come here tonight because I was nervous too. Before I came, I decided to say yes to opportunities. I said yes to you, and I'm very glad I did."

The man held Marjorie's arm and whispered, "Thank you."

Marjorie slowly nodded, never expecting something like this to happen, and he watched her walk away.

In her apartment, she sat in the overstuffed, white chair near the window and watched her own gossamer curtains dance in the summer breeze.

She thought about the man and smiled. She couldn't remember ever having a better time with a stranger. Something in his eyes warmed her heart, and she wanted to know him better.

As the man walked home, he thought about Marjorie and smiled. He couldn't remember ever having a better time with a stranger. Something in her eyes warmed his heart, and he wanted to know her better.

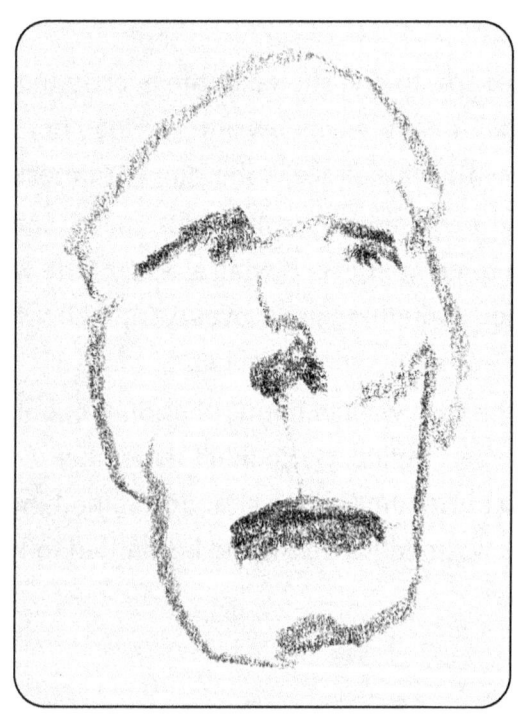

49-4

MALCOLM BARNHOUSE

Even though he was approaching 90 years old, Malcolm Barnhouse didn't have any wrinkles on his face. His lips formed a straight line, and his nose looked like a red button.

His face was long and thin, and the unblemished skin was taut. It was almost as if he was wearing a mask, like the Phantom of the Opera.

His blank expression rarely changed, regardless of the situation.

Actually, one thing that *did* change was the area around his eyes. When he was concerned about something, he would look up slightly and to the left, furrowing his eyebrows.

One day, Malcolm heard a knock on his front door. He wheeled himself to the living room to see who it was and peeked through the curtains.

"Mr. Barnhouse? Are you Mr. Barnhouse?"

"Yes?"

"May we come in?"

Malcolm squinted to see who "we" was. A woman and a man were standing at the door with clipboards.

"Clipboards," he thought. "That's trouble."

"What do you want?" he yelled to the strangers.

"Well, Mr. Barnhouse, we are from the insurance company. Since your house is insured with us, you are hereby mandated to purchase a new roof. We can no longer insure your house with this roof."

The woman and the man stood in the doorway, waiting for a response.

Sitting in his wheelchair, Malcolm displayed his usual blank expression, straight-across lips, and furrowed brow, and his blood began to boil.

"May we come in?" they repeated politely.

"No, you may not!" he shouted at the closed door. "I cannot afford a new roof. I am an old man, and I live alone. This roof will outlive me!"

"Well, Mr. Barnhouse ... we've tried to reach you several times by e-mail, regular mail, and phone, so this was our last attempt to connect with you."

"My wife used to do all the connecting for the both of us, but now I don't do any of it. I'm just trying to get by with what I've got in the time I have left."

Malcolm heard the woman and the man ask each other what to do. Finally, Malcolm saw their business card appear under the door.

He didn't know what was going to happen about the roof, but he really didn't care. The roof would be added to a long list of things he avoided since his wife died. She had always meant to teach him how to manage their affairs, but that day never came.

Through the curtains, Malcolm watched the clipboard couple walk away.

He wheeled himself in front of the television and ate the cold sandwich that he had made a couple of hours before.

He glanced at the mirror across the room and saw his reflection.

"Old, grumpy man in a wheelchair," he mumbled. "Yep. My wife was right about me after all."

74-5

ATTICUS FARMER

he three children looked up at their grandpa, who was telling a story from his favorite chair by the fire.

"When I was a little boy ..."

The children waited for the rest of the sentence, but it didn't come. It wasn't the first time that Atticus Farmer had nodded off like that; after all, he was 99 years old.

"There he goes again," whispered Little Larry. "I wonder what he's thinking about."

"Maybe he's thinking about the farm where he grew up," said Timid Timmy.

Still waiting, the children's legs were getting numb after sitting cross-legged on the floor for so long.

Atticus suddenly opened his eyes, and he spoke to the space above the children's heads:

"When I was a little boy during the Great Depression, our farm produced more crops than anyone could afford to buy. Prices fell, factories closed, and our workers were laid off. We couldn't pay off our bank loan, and we lost the farm in foreclosure."

The three children stared at their grandpa. Although they had no idea what his words meant, they knew that he was remembering a very hard time.

Darling Donna told her mother that their grandpa wasn't making any sense.

"Oh, I've heard these stories before," her mother explained. "On days when my dad's mind is clear and calm, these old memories come up. When he closes his eyes, he always goes back to the farm. Even though it was a hard time, it was his happy place—before everything turned bad, of course."

As the other two children watched their grandpa snooze, Little Larry whispered, "I wonder what it was like to live on that farm."

"Grandpa had five brothers and four sisters," Timid Timmy told him, "and they all lived in a two-room house."

"Wow!" Darling Donna added. "We sure have it good now. Don't we, Momma?"

"Yes, we do indeed."

Atticus barely heard these conversations because he was tending oats, sorghum, alfalfa, and corn, and his back ached from bending. He smelled the bread—made with flour, yeast, salt, and water—that his mother had just baked in their humble fireplace, and he heard the goats bleat in the distance.

The call of "Dinner!" brought him out of his reverie.

Atticus opened his eyes and slowly stood up. His usual seat at the head of the table was waiting for him, and he shuffled toward it. Everyone else was seated.

With a confused look on his wrinkled face, he shouted, "Who the hell ARE you people?"

The three children and their mother exchanged uncomfortable glances and looked at their plates.

After a few silent moments, Atticus sat down, clumsily picked up his soup spoon, and loudly slurped.

72-1

NANA HELEN

hen I was a little girl—maybe 10 years old—I spent the night at my grandmother's house.

My parents dropped me off, and Nana Helen and I sat in her living room in silence for what seemed like an eternity. When I finally glanced in her direction, I saw that she had dozed off.

I looked at her gray, short hair, and her gray-tinted eyeglasses. She was frail, and her pale skin seemed translucent.

A car horn startled her awake, and she looked in my direction.

"Who's there?" she growled.

"It's me, Nana."

"What are *you* doing here?"

"I'm going to stay with you tonight."

"Well, nobody told me anything about *that*. I should have at least been consulted!"

Nana Helen became blind at an early age, soon after marrying my grandfather. After he passed away, she lived alone.

Before this day, I had few memories of her, and the ones I did have were not pleasant. She rarely talked at family get-togethers and, when she did, she barked orders at anyone in the room.

Nana stood up and expertly felt her way into the kitchen. She was the only blind person I had ever seen up close, and I was fascinated with her skills in knowing where everything was.

After I was seated at her small kitchen table, she carefully poured cereal into two bowls, added milk to each, and placed one bowl in front of me.

We sat with the light off, and the only sound I heard was our chewing.

Suddenly, she asked, "Do you know how I became blind?"

"No, Nana."

"Detached retina. No money for a doctor."

Nana let out a big sigh and turned her head to face me.

"After I lost my sight, I became bitter, sad, afraid, and mad at the world. I never used to be this way. I used to have fun. I was kind to people. My favorite thing in life was giving my love to others. I guess that's why your grandfather fell in love with me."

I had never seen this side of her.

"Why can't you be like you were before?"

She took off her dark glasses and wiped away the tears.

"Well, dear, I guess I forgot how."

"I'll teach you, Nana!"

The rest of the night was wonderful. We laughed, told jokes, sang songs, and gave our hearts to each other.

When my parents came to pick me up the next morning, they said, "Go and say goodbye to your grandmother."

I approached Nana and touched her arm. She reached in her pocket, pulled out a locket that belonged to her mother, and gave it to me.

Pulling me close to her, she whispered, "I love you, dear. Thank you."

After that day, the family noticed something different about Nana, but no one knew what it was or what had caused it.

I haven't told anyone about it until now.

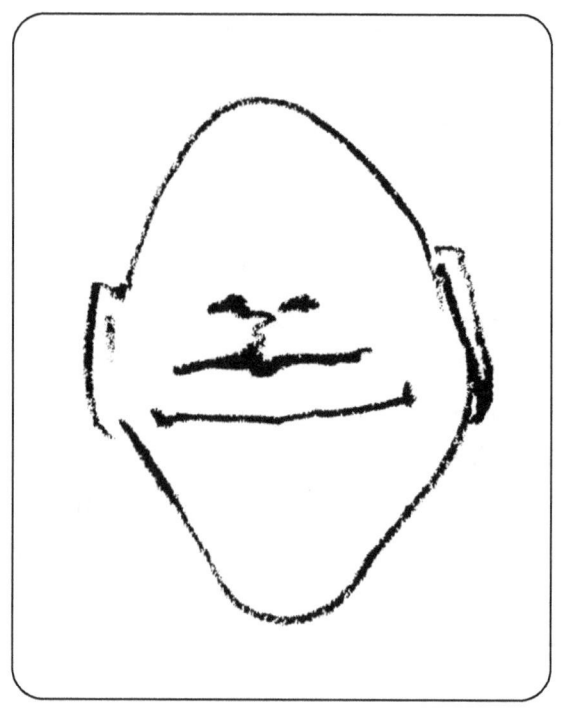

103-1

HAPPY CAMPER

onald "Happy" Camper found love. He wasn't looking for it, but apparently it was looking for him.

On an early-morning stroll through his favorite neighborhood park, Ronald listened to the birds tweet-tweet, said "howdy-do" to the passers-by, and breathed in the cool air.

His straight-across grin was relaxed and gentle, and his eyes were friendly-looking.

Before he went to bed every night, he thanked the universe for the amazing gift of his life.

Ronald was content with his solitary existence. His friends gave him the nickname "Happy" because it fit his good mood and it was funny when said with his last name.

In the park, Ronald took a path through a dense crop of weeping cherry trees. Their showy pink blossoms contrasted beautifully with the lush green grass beneath them.

He sat on a wooden bench and began to read the newspaper. Looking up and to the left, he noticed a flash of bright yellow in the near distance. Even though he squinted his eyes, he couldn't figure out what it was, which piqued his curiosity even more. (He was a very curious fellow.)

The yellow object moved closer and closer, and Ronald was riveted. *What was it?*

After a few minutes, the mystery was solved.

A woman was standing in front of him. She had blond hair and wore a yellow dress, a yellow hat, and shiny yellow shoes.

"May I join you?" she politely asked.

Ronald jumped up and said, "Why, of *course* you may!"

Jasmine sat on the bench and looked at the cherry trees. Ronald sat beside her and resumed reading his newspaper. It felt comfortable for both of them.

On most days, Ronald and Jasmine met at the same park bench.

Arm in arm, they would stroll through the beautiful park regardless of the weather. They enjoyed the fresh air and each other's conversation. They talked about the past, the present, and the future with transparency and ease.

To the unknowing eye, Ronald's face looked the same—relaxed and gentle—but he knew that there was a difference between his old life and this new one.

On this day, Ronald and Jasmine met at the park bench as usual, and she had an apprehensive look on her face.

"What's wrong, my dear?"

"Nothing's wrong, Happy. I have something to ask you."

"You can ask me anything."

Jasmine took a deep breath, knelt on one knee, and whispered, *"Will you marry me?"*

Ronald's eyes watered, which hadn't happened in a very long time. His face flushed, and his grin, which usually went across his whole face, seemed to get even wider.

"Yes, Jasmine. I will."

Ronald was a very happy camper.

CARPET CREATURES
YARN SCRAPS

CARPET CREATURES PROJECT

It all started with a carpet and a sketch pad. You can read more about this project at taegallery.com/carpet-creatures.

YARN SCRAPS NEWSLETTER

Our Yarn Scraps newsletter showcases and shares writings about our Carpet Creatures.

To view the latest version of Yarn Scraps, visit taegallery.com/carpet-creatures and select **"Link to Yarn Scraps newsletter (latest edition)."**

WRITE, WRITE, WRITE

To be a part of Yarn Scraps, select images from the Carpet Creatures catalog (taegallery.com/carpet-creatures/catalog) and write your reactions to them.

Write stories, poems, captions, or other thoughts in whatever format you choose, and add titles if you wish.

SEND, SEND, SEND

E-mail your writing (with catalog numbers) to carpetcreatures@taegallery.com.

When we include your writing and byline in Yarn Scraps, we'll suggest minor and complimentary editorial revisions and send you the revised text for your approval.

Feel free to send the newsletter to anyone you know (of any age), so they can join in the Carpet Creatures fun.

Think of Yarn Scraps as a "book in the making," and we'll watch it grow together.

A GIFT FOR YOU

As a thank-you gift for participating, you'll receive a copy of this book

MOST OF ALL ...

Have fun and be creative!